UNDERNEATH THE SIDEWALK

CLAIRE EAMER   THOMAS GIBAULT

North Winds Press
An Imprint of Scholastic Canada Ltd.

The illustrations for this book are digital paintings.
The text type is set in 26 point Filosofia.

Library and Archives Canada Cataloguing in Publication
Eamer, Claire, 1947-, author
Underneath the sidewalk / written by Claire Eamer;
illustrated by Thomas Gibault.

ISBN 978-1-4431-4636-4 (hardback)

I. Gibault, Thomas, 1982-, illustrator II. Title.

PS8609.A53U64 2016   jC813'.6   C2016-901614-5

www.scholastic.ca

6 5 4 3 2 1   Printed in Malaysia   108   16 17 18 19 20

For a small boy in Whitehorse who was worried about sidewalk cracks, and for Patrick who played with many beasts.
— C.E.

To Sanam-joon.
— T.G.

Run, jump, spin round,
Skipping to the playground.

Skip, hop, jump, stop!
Crack in the sidewalk.

Dark crack, deep crack,
Down-below-the-street crack.

Don't slip, don't slide,
Down to the dark side.

Dark side, down side,
That's where the beasts hide.

Claws grope, teeth clack,
Just below the dark crack.

Safe now, at the park,
No cracks, no dark.

Run, jump, slip-slide,
Mom seeks, I hide.

Swing low, swing high,
Swing to the blue sky.

We romp, we play,
Best-day-of-all day!

Home time, skip, hop,
Back along the sidewalk.

Run, skip, jump – smack!
Down through a big crack.

Rumble, tumble, scrape, bump,
Land with a loud thump.

"OW!"

Dark there, everywhere,
Deep in the beasts' lair.

No sound, no peep.
Maybe they're all asleep?

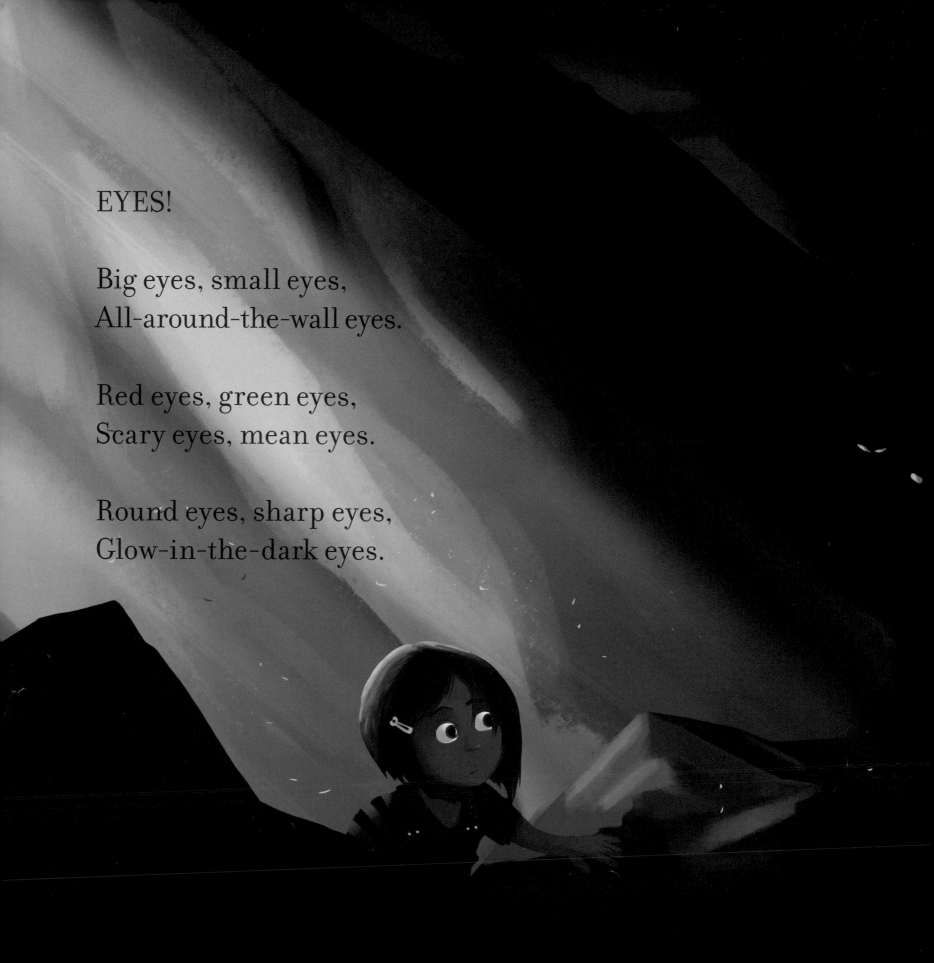

EYES!

Big eyes, small eyes,
All-around-the-wall eyes.

Red eyes, green eyes,
Scary eyes, mean eyes.

Round eyes, sharp eyes,
Glow-in-the-dark eyes.

Tall beast, small beast,
Tooth-fang-and-claw beast!

Eyes glare, teeth flash,
Fangs gleam, tails lash.

Claw scrapes across the floor,
More eyes, and even more.

Hot breath on my hair,
Claws, eyes everywhere.

All around, all about,
Till I shout a mighty
SHOUT . . .

Mouths shut, eyes blink,
Claws hide, tails sink.

Scared beast, sad beast,
Maybe-not-so-bad beast?

Little beast, small voice,
Bravest-one-of-all voice:

"Hello . . .
Do you want to play?"

Run, jump, skip, hop,
Home along the sidewalk.

Cracks don't scare me,
I know what I'll see,

Deep in the dark side,
Down where my friends hide.

I'll go back there,
Back to the beasts' lair.

Run, jump, skip, hop,
Underneath the sidewalk.